Competition in Africa

Pilar Palacià

illustrated by
Manohar B Jadhav

Competition in Africa

Unisun Publications
Unisun Technologies (P) Ltd,
7, Floor-1, Kodava Samaja Building,
First Main Road, Vasanthnagar, Bangalore 560052, India.
Phone: 91-80-22289290 Fax: 91-80-22289294.
e-mail: info@unisun4writers.com
website www.unisun4writers.com

First print: December 2005

Typeset and printed by Ad Prints and Publishers
2/1, 3rd Cross, Mysore Road, Bangalore, India.

Special Indian Price: Rs 125/- only

ISBN 81-88234-17-6

Dedication

To my five beloved little ones . . .

Acknowledgements

I would like to thank,
My friend, Dr Malavika Kapur, for all her help and support.
Annie Chandy Mathew, Meenakshi Varma and
Sasha Maria from Team Unisun.

CONTENTS

COMPETITION IN AFRICA

Aisha the glow-worm was really worried about the decision she had to make in a few hours. She had been chosen as leader of the school team and had to select her team members for the competition.

It was still early in the morning. Squatting on top of a rock, she wondered how much time she had before her mother called her for breakfast. It's amazing how little sleep you get when you have to make a tough decision, she thought.

She remembered only two groups had made it to the Palace of Wonders the previous year but none could solve the riddle to open the door. It was imperative that she should make the right choices. The problem was that the team leader was not given the rules of the game beforehand. So she had to choose her team without knowing what lay ahead or what challenges they would have to face. That was going to be tough.

Last year's leader from school had chosen the fastest athletes, but they lost out in the riddle test. Their minds had not been fast enough. It was obvious that speed and strength were not sufficient. What was it, then? She had lain awake thinking about it all night. In desperation, she decided the best thing to do would be to hop out of bed and visit the Wise Shaman.

She got up, put on her purple gloves and red hat. Careful not to wake the rest of the family, she crawled away from her rocky home towards the Old Oak, where the Wise Shaman had lived for the last hundred years or more.

She was nervous because everyone knew that even though the Wise Shaman was very kind, he almost always answered a question with a question. He would just keep on asking questions when one desperately wanted answers! Aisha was a little worried she wouldn't be able to answer any of his questions. And if she couldn't, then how would she ever know?

When she arrived at the Old Oak, she saw the Wise Shaman perched on a branch gazing at the disappearing stars. He was quiet as always, and all Aisha could see were his huge brown eyes. He seemed all eyes. Eyes that seemed to see everything and a small beak that would seldom open. He opened it only to say wise things. He was indeed the wisest creature around.

"Greetings Wise Shaman," Aisha called. The Wise Shaman bent his gaze on her.

"Who calls upon the Wise Shaman?" he boomed. Aisha wobbled a little. "Aisha the glow-worm, Shaman Sir," she replied unsteadily.

"And what brings you here so early, little lady?" he asked, softer now as he spied the charming little glow-worm below in a red hat and purple gloves.

"Wise Shaman, I know you can help me and today I really need your help," said Aisha.

"Tell me young lady," the Wise Shaman said, flying down to meet her. "What's bothering you?"

"I need to choose the members of my team in a few hours, and I don't know what to do," Aisha said anxiously.

"Why do you need to do that?" the Wise Shaman asked.

"Because we'll be competing against teams from other schools here in Africa, and we really want to win."

"And why do you want to win?" he asked.

Aisha had not expected that. She had never thought about that. After all, everyone always wanted to win.

"If I didn't win, I'd lose, right?" she said after a moment's pause. "Then I'd be like everybody else. But I want to be the one to win. Doesn't everyone?" She paused. "And now that I think about it, I'm also curious about what lies inside the Palace of Wonders."

"And why do you want to know what is inside that Palace?" came the next question.

"Because it must be something very interesting and the judges have said it's something worth knowing. I like to know things... like how Africa truly is... and I am curious," she confessed.

"What are the rules of the game?" the Wise Shaman asked.

"That's the problem," Aisha answered. "Nobody knows the rules. So how am I going to choose my team members when I don't even know what we'll have to do?"

The Wise Shaman closed his eyes. When he reopened them he said:

"So it sounds like an adventure doesn't it?"

"Yeah! Sure it does," Aisha said.

"So, if you were going on an adventure, who would you like to take with you?"

"That's easy," Aisha answered. "My friends of course. But… most of them are bad at competitions."

"But if you don't know the rules yet, what difference does that make?"

"You're right," Aisha said reluctantly.

"When you don't know what lies ahead, wouldn't you rather have a friend with you?"

Aisha was thinking how true that was, when the Wise Shaman added one final question, "What do you do when you have a really tough decision to make and you don't know what to do?"

"Then I just do what I feel is right," Aisha burst out, not quite sure she knew what she meant.

"So you follow the dictates of your heart, huh?" He shut his big eyes firmly. And Aisha knew he would not say another word.

Aisha inched away from the Old Oak. It was still dark. She thought of the last exchange with the Wise Shaman. Listening to one's heart sounded like the easiest thing to do, but she had never really known her heart could speak. Come to think of it, she had not really thought seriously about her heart or what it might have to say. She made up her mind to find out more. When she got home, her mother was cooking breakfast. The smell was so delicious, that Aisha felt better right away. Breakfast was usually just a plain green shake but today her mother had added fruit-fly extract. It was delicious.

She told her mother all about the visit to the Wise Shaman over breakfast.

"Can one's heart speak, mama?" she asked plaintively.

"It certainly does, baby," Aisha's mother said with conviction. "And you're sure to hear it when it speaks to you. Now be off quickly, or you'll be late for school."

Aisha climbed into the school bus. Unlike many other schools, hers accepted all kinds of students. Her bus was an elephant-foot leaf pulled by Mr Swift. Everyone loved Mr Swift, a kind and jolly rabbit.

Aisha usually enjoyed her long ride to school. But today, she was thankful that she was the last to get on the bus. That meant Mr Swift would go straight to school.

Everyone on the bus was excited about the competition. They were depending on Aisha to win. It was a great responsibility for her. She had to choose the right team members to win. Every year the contest was different, but everyone seemed to fail at some point or the other and nobody had been able to win so far, though the Ministry of Education had implemented the annual event twelve years ago. Maybe Aisha would be the first one.

Aisha was the tiniest glow-worm at school. She was always very quiet, but she participated in everything. So, despite being so quiet, she had many friends.

Everybody normally tumbled out of the school bus, racing to make it on time before the Big Bell went. Aisha usually waited for the bus to empty before she scrambled out. She was always a little careful, since the other students were all so much bigger than her.

But today, it was different. When the bus reached school, everyone let her go out first.

"Good luck, Aisha," they called out.

Mr Swift tousled her head and said warmly, "Good luck, kid. Do us all proud."

Aisha headed for the library to wait there while everyone else flew towards the schoolyard.

11

Finally, the moment had arrived... the most difficult moment of Aisha's young life. She knew she had to make a choice that would mean victory or defeat for the school team, and she felt the weight of the responsibility.

Excited, she went to the podium where she had to call out the names of the team members on the microphone. She had never used a microphone before.

She remembered the Wise Shaman's last question. "So you follow the dictates of your heart, huh?" His answers were always questions. Was that his way of telling her what to do? She decided to do as he seemed to suggest. She didn't know the rules of the game as yet. So she might as well go ahead, surrounded by friends who loved her and accepted her.

There was a sudden hush and Ms Rosie Rigorous arrived... with the dignity and authority of all flamingos. Fixing everyone with a stern eye, she pushed her tiny steel-framed glasses further back on her long beak, and read aloud.

"Dear students," she said, "We are gathered here this morning to witness the selection of the team members who will represent our school this year at the most important competition in Africa. We are aware there has never been a winner, but we are still optimistic. I only ask our team to do their best. The first instructions will be given once the teams are presented to the judges."

"This year," she continued, "the Board of Teachers has chosen Aisha to lead our team. We'd like to assure her of our wholehearted support."

Aisha could feel all eyes on her. Smiling bravely, she lifted her chin a little. Ms Rigorous finally nodded and said, "Aisha, you may begin. Remember once you select a team mate, you cannot change your mind."

Aisha looked around. She saw some of the best students and some of the best athletes. Her mind told her that her heart would choose a strange group, but she decided to go ahead anyway.

"Fani Talltale," Aisha called.

Fani the giraffe was surprised. She was sure she had not heard correctly. She must be daydreaming again. She was awful at sports. Her neck was so long, most of the time she was not aware of what was going on in the game anyway.

What Fani loved to do was tell tall tales. She always had her head up in the clouds and always had a story to tell. Fani had not expected Aisha to choose her but she was really glad she did.

Everybody turned to look at the slender giraffe as she sprinted towards the podium, smiling broadly.

"Larry Shortsight, please."

Larry the rhino was thrilled. He walked towards the podium, careful not to hurt anybody with his front horn. That front horn could be a bother sometimes; it prevented him seeing anything more than three feet ahead of him. But secretly, he was quite proud of his horn, as all rhinos are.

"Who's next?"

While Aisha thought, Sprint the leopard fumed. A team including a nearly blind animal and a silly dreamer was going to take Aisha nowhere. If only they had chosen him as leader! As an athlete, he knew best. It was all about being the fastest.

"James Playful," Aisha yelled.

Jumpy James the monkey, or JJ, as he was called, was getting a little restless with the ceremony. But he perked up when he heard his name called and crept slowly towards the podium hoping Ms Rigorous would not notice that he had not been paying attention.

Mabel Carusina was called out next.

Mabel the deer was Aisha's best friend. She was the star of the school choir. Maybe there was a singing section to the competition, she thought. This could be her chance to be famous! Everyone looked at her admiringly as she dashed past. She was so pretty with her lovely brown eyes and soft voice. She was indeed popular, but nobody admired her more than Yago. He simply could not take his eyes off her, but he was too shy to let anyone know of his feelings, especially Mabel herself.

Aisha was getting nervous. Was she right in choosing teammates, all so different from each other? However, she decided to go on. After all, even if they lost, they would still have good memories of their time together.

"Steven Xai."

Steven Xai the panda was an exchange student from China. He missed the wet climate of the Far East and was still having trouble settling down. But he was Aisha's friend. And if she wanted him there, he wasn't about to let her down.

"Aisha," Ms Rigorous said, "with the next member you choose, you will have half your team. Continue."

"Yes, ma'am. I choose Christy Herby."

Christy the snake almost tumbled over in surprise. She was usually left out of most activities because she was diabetic. She was so excited, that she began to plan a special dish for the team to celebrate their getting together. No sugar in it, of course.

Sprint the leopard was furious. Was Aisha not planning to choose him? They were friends and Aisha knew how good he was. Instead, here she was, choosing all those other students! Aisha's tiny voice was heard just then, announcing another name.

"Roy Trombone."

Roy trumpeted in joy. Everyone skipped out of his way as he walked to the podium. He was a clumsy elephant and when delighted, he could be very

destructive, without meaning to, of course. However he managed not to hurt anyone this time.

"Sprint Fast," Aisha said with a smile.

"Finally," Sprint thought. This was such an odd bunch though. But maybe that wasn't such a bad thing. After all, in anything to do with sports, nobody could beat him. This could be his chance to really shine.

He could see his picture splashed across the cover page of *Animal Times* with a caption saying 'Sprint, the Fast'.

"Who's next, Aisha?"

"Croquie Belle."

Sprint almost had a heart attack. What on earth was Aisha thinking? Croquie was probably the slowest animal at school. He suddenly understood why Aisha had mentioned him before Croquie. He would never have accepted if Croquie had already been in the team.

Croquie crawled up to the podium, applauded by all the other crocodiles. She looked sadly at Mabel, as she passed, wishing she were half as lovely as the slim deer.

Croquie took her place on the podium, careful that she was as far away from Sprint as possible. She shrank under his glare.

"You require two more members, Aisha. Go ahead," said Ms Rigorous.

"Yes, I want Choo-Choo Goodeye and Yago Heartful in the team."

Choo-Choo flew to her place among the members of the team. She was not a bright eagle, and often required help from Aisha with her schoolwork but she was eager to do her bit.

Yago the beaver was another foreign student. He belonged to the wetlands of Russia where his favorite activity was building dams. He couldn't see how he would be of use to the team but he realized he would be near Mabel Carusina and that meant heaven for him. If only he didn't have such big teeth! But then, all beavers had big teeth. He couldn't change that.

Ms Rigorous looked at the assorted group and smiled faintly. Addressing the group, she said, "You will be representing our school in the most important contest in the region. Do your best. Never give up, no matter how tough the going may get. It is always better to risk and lose rather than not take the risk at all. Tomorrow at sunrise, you will meet the other teams at the porch of the Palace of Wonders. There you will be given your first instructions. Rest today. You have a difficult week ahead of you. Good luck."

Everyone applauded and cheered. The Game would soon begin!

Aisha was glad she had chosen her best friends, and she realized that hers was a very mixed team. Larry, Steven and she, were good students, but Larry was myopic; Steven lacked fluency with language and she herself was really tiny. Mabel was the star of the choir and Fani was good at spinning yarns, but they were only interested in those things; Roy was the band-leader, but he was so clumsy sometimes, that it was dangerous to be within striking distance of him; Choo-Choo could find anything at a great distance with her big, beautiful eyes, and was great at fishing, but she was a slow learner.

Christy was a great cook, and knew a lot about healing with herbs, but she was diabetic and Aisha was a little worried about whether she could handle much physical strain. Yago was a good student and a generous fellow, but he was so shy that he seemed aggressive at times; Croquie was a great swimmer, but she was painfully slow on land; James was excellent at developing strategies, but he only wanted to play all the time and Sprint was the best athlete at school, but he was arrogant and impatient with anybody who was slower than him.

But they all had one thing in common: they had good hearts and they were her friends.

Day One

The morning of the competition dawned fine and bright. All six teams had assembled by the porch of the Palace of Wonders.

The first team was full of feline athletes. They looked confident of victory. The second team consisted of huge elephants. They would certainly win if the competition depended on strength. Cold-blooded animals formed the third team. They would never get into a panic and lose their cool.

The fourth group was the flying team. The fifth consisted of small animals, like rabbits, and foxes. The sixth was Aisha's team. All the other teams seemed to have uniformity while hers seemed a mixed and motley crew.

The excitement was palpable as the six team-leaders approached the judges who handed them envelopes with their first directions. The oldest judge, a turtle, addressed them in a deep, solemn voice.

"You have been given an envelope with your first instructions now. You will receive your next set of instructions once you achieve the first goal, and so on. Good luck to all of you and may the best team win."

Aisha went to her team, opened the first envelope and read.

"Get to the Singing Spring as fast as we call.
Remember: all together or none at all."

Aisha knew how tough that could be. Especially for a team like hers. And this was only the first hurdle! She decided to discuss it with Jumpy James. He was always full of ideas and strategies.

Jumpy James thought of something immediately. "Steven can take you and Christy. Larry can take Yago and me. The real problem is Croquie. But we can just build a platform for her and Roy can pull it."

Sprint said it would take forever and Yago said it would be too much work but Choo-Choo scoured the horizon and spied an old wooden plank they could use.

Jumpy James then cut two vines
as cords, tied one end to Roy's body, and the
other to the plank. Once it was secured firmly, Croquie
crawled on to it and they set off. But they were very slow, despite
the 'invention'. So Choo-Choo was sent off to spy on the other teams.

She returned with the following report. "The flying team was the first to
arrive. The felines arrived next. Both have already got their second envelope and
are on their way. The cold-blooded group is not far behind, and following them
are the elephants. A little ahead of us is the team with the small animals, which
means we're in last place. I'm sorry, folks. We'll just have to move faster."

They were all disappointed. Christy, knowing how important morale was for
a team, asked Mabel to sing.

"Come on, Mabel. Sing a song," she pleaded.

Mabel hesitated, but then Christy chanted the following words.

> "Sing a song
> As you hop along,
> And every mile,
> Will be worth your while."

18

Sprint thought singing was a sheer waste of time. He was always more focused on getting somewhere rather than on the joy of the journey.

However, once Roy began to toot on his trunk and Mabel began to sing a song, they began to feel like they were on a picnic. And before they knew it, they had arrived at the Singing Spring.

The Singing Spring, in fact was doing just that. It sang a song as it bubbled along, which was why it flowed along so merrily. Aisha noticed that the spring was trying to whisper its joyous message, a message the team had learnt from experience.

Choo-Choo spied their envelope right away. Unfortunately it was the only one there, which meant all the other teams were already ahead. The envelope had a card with the following message:

"Get to the bridge across the fall,
All for one... and one for all.
First key: You are beautiful the way you are."

"What does that mean?" Fani asked.

"Maybe that's a key to a riddle," Aisha said. "They want us to find out who is beautiful the way he or she is."

Croquie said what everyone was thinking, "That's easy: Mabel."

"O no!" said Mabel shy, but pleased. "They must mean someone famous, maybe a great singer."

"Well," Aisha said, "we'll sleep on it and begin early tomorrow. But let's not forget we're still in last place. Good night, everyone."

They all went to sleep a little frustrated because they were lagging so far behind. Sprint glared at Croquie, but said nothing. He was not used to coming last. Poor Croquie squirmed. Maybe if she stayed behind, the team would be able to move faster. She didn't want to be a burden. She made up her mind to talk to Aisha about it, first thing next morning.

Day Two

"No, Croquie, we will not leave you behind. I chose you and we're all in this together," Aisha said when Croquie tackled her about it.

"But Aisha," Croquie said, "I'm just slowing you down. There's no point in keeping me."

"All for one and one for all," Aisha said firmly.

"I don't know," said Croquie with an uncertain smile, "but if you want me, I'll be there."

"Thank you, Croquie. Now let's wake everyone up. We have to make up for lost time."

Christy prepared a delicious breakfast. Nobody could figure out what she put in it. And she would never say. She only smiled and said it was a very old recipe, very nutritious and full of energy-boosters. After breakfast, the team began their journey towards the fall.

Sprint began to get restless, longing to shoot off at his own speed. Jumpy James could see that Sprint hated having to wait for the others to catch up. He decided to do something about that.

"Hey Sprint," he called. "I bet you can't get to the fall and back under three hours."

"Just watch me," Sprint retorted, shooting off at a tremendous speed. Ah! Finally, he could keep his own pace.

Once he left, Croquie felt a little more comfortable and decided to enjoy the ride. Soon, they were all singing and Mabel explained her plan to form a band from among the team members.

That alarmed Yago. He had a dreadful voice and knew it. But he simply could not refuse Mabel.

"You know, Mabel," he said, "if you really want to have a choir, you'll need an audience too, somebody who'll listen and point out all the errors. I could do that."

Everyone laughed at this, considering Yago had such a terrible ear for music. He smiled. What a difference a little humor made! Maybe he should try this more often, he thought.

Two and a half hours later, Sprint returned. He looked grave.

"Wow!" said Jumpy James "You made it. You're super fast."

"Thanks, JJ," Sprint replied. "But I have bad news. Four groups are already on the other side of the fall. The flying team did not need the bridge, and the small animals and cold-blooded team crossed it easily. However, the felines, destroyed part of the bridge to prevent the elephants from crossing. The elephants are going down to check whether they can cross where the waterfall ends. But, they'll take forever, so I doubt they'll make it. As for our team, we have Roy, Steven and Larry. And they're heavy."

"I know," said Aisha, "let's hurry and we'll decide once we get there."

They kept going, but had lost their earlier cheerfulness. Roy, in particular, felt really bad because he was the heaviest. However, nobody knew there was someone far more nervous: Mabel. She was afraid of heights and could not imagine crossing a bridge above a fall.

They got to the bridge at last.

"Isn't it beautiful?" Fani cried. "I love that rainbow over the fall."

Everyone looked where Fani was pointing. It was indeed breathtaking. But soon they caught sight of the damaged bridge. The narrow wooden bridge was tied to three of the four corners by vines, but the fourth had been destroyed by the felines. It would not bear the weight of a heavy animal.

"We'll just have to fix it," JJ said, spelling out what everyone else was thinking. "Yago, help me cut a vine. We'll use it to tie up the loose end. The knot will have to be extra tight. Christy, with your knowledge of herbs, can you cook up something to strengthen the ropes?"

"I'll try," said Christy, wondering what she could possibly strengthen the ropes with.

"Okay guys, let's get to work."

Everybody got started. Except Mabel. She did not want to cross the bridge at all. She did not even dare to look down to calculate the distance.

Yago went up Fani's neck to cut some vines with his teeth. In the meantime, Christy cooked up some sticky substance, which she applied to the vine. The vine was then used to tie the fourth end of the bridge with Choo-Choo's help.

Roy and Steven between themselves hauled up a log and threw it onto on the bridge to test its strength. It held, as they had all hoped. The knot was very strong.

Roy decided to cross. It was now or never. Steven watched him, his heart beating loudly. Mabel watched through a chink between her fingers. She was too frightened to even uncover her face.

Christy and Choo-Choo were already on the other side, waiting. Aisha felt responsible for the group, so she decided to cross with Roy. They crossed over slowly. Sweat poured down Roy's forehead. He knew he was not only heavy but clumsy too. He was always stepping on someone or breaking something, and he certainly did not want to break the bridge. Aisha knew how Roy was feeling, so she encouraged him until they were safe on the other side.

Everyone cheered. They felt more courageous now. Sprint decided to go next, and Fani and Croquie followed him. Fani knew Croquie would take ages, so she started to spin a yarn.

"Once upon a time, Croquie, there was this pirate who needed to cross a very long bridge to reach an enormous treasure. The problem was that he would take longer than a day to cross it, but by then the tide would rise and he would drown. He did not know what to do but he really wanted the treasure. He thought, if someone had put the treasure there, it meant it was possible to cross. So what do you think he did?" Fani asked.

"I have no idea, Fani, you're the one with the imagination," Croquie answered. She was moving very slowly, but by now she was already drawn into the tale. "I would've swum. Couldn't the pirate swim?"

"No, my dear Croquie, he was scared of the water."

"So," Croquie asked, "what did he do?"

"Well, there were two very friendly crocodiles who had lost their jobs. So, he hired them to pull a plank to get to the other shore and come back. Money and

jewels meant nothing to the crocodiles, so they were happy with airline tickets to a wonderful tropical swamp."

"Wow!" Croquie cried, "I love swamps. Did the pirate make it?"

"Yes, Croquie, he crossed just like we have."

"Yeah!" everyone else shouted. Two more on the other side!

Steven and James went together next. They were very different, but they had begun learning from one another. Steven was always studying, while James was out playing. So they decided that they would help each other. They struck a deal: James would get to like books and Steven would learn to have fun playing outside. It was to begin as soon as they went back to school.

Then it was Larry the rhino's turn. He was anxious. Choo-Choo immediately understood how he was feeling and flew back to him.

"Larry, it's now your turn to cross. I will be your eyes and guide you."

"Thank you Choo-Choo," Larry said. "I was really worried… you know I can't see too well."

So Choo-Choo guided Larry and they crossed easily because Larry felt more confident now.

Only Mabel and Yago remained on the other side. Mabel began to cry. "I'm sorry guys," she said tearfully, "I dare not cross. I'm petrified. Go ahead without me."

"Oh no!" Yago shouted just then. "We're never going to make it if this little princess sits around making a fuss."

Outraged at Yago's sharp tone, Mabel cried, "Who do you think you are, you nasty little beaver? I can do whatever I jolly well want."

"Then how come, for all your snobbishness you can't even cross a simple bridge?" Yago yelled, beginning to walk backwards toward the bridge, "At least I'm not a coward like you!"

Mabel was so angry she did not realize she had started to follow Yago across the bridge. "Well, let me tell you something, you rude beaver! At least, I try and cheer folks up with my music. I'm not ill behaved like you are! You're just plain mean and you hurt people's feelings."

"Bah!" Yago spat… all the while, walking backwards as slowly as he could. He wasn't quite sure what he was saying. He only was trying to distract Mabel as much as he could so that she wouldn't notice where she was. "You don't even sing, you whine," he taunted her.

"Oh!" cried Mabel, furious. Yago had touched a sensitive spot. "How dare you! I'm the best singer at school."

She was suddenly cut off by the sound of clapping. Looking up, she saw the rest of the group in front of her. She was surprised.

"I'm sorry Mabel," Yago said softly. "I had to make you angry so you'd get distracted and cross the bridge without even knowing what you were doing. I didn't mean what I said. I think you sing beautifully."

Mabel was so touched she almost wept. She realized that Yago had been a hero. He had been so brave, walking backwards. She did not know what to say. All she did was stoop and kiss Yago's cheek. Yago was thrilled.

Everybody shouted, kissing and hugging the friend who had helped him or her cross. Only Sprint felt a little left out, because even though he was just as happy as the others, he had not helped anyone. He began to feel he was missing out on something.

"Now that we're all together again, let's look for our envelope," Aisha said.

Once again, Choo-Choo found the envelope. Aisha opened it and read:

"To Grizzly Mountain you must go,
To find the Golden Tree.
Once you get there, you will know,
While all the stones are very pretty.
The ones for you and your team
Are yellow, purple and leafy green.
Second key: Where you are... is where you should be."

"Eh? What's that about the second key," Larry asked. "Is it part of the same riddle, or a different one?"

"I have the feeling it's like part of a puzzle. They're all little bits of a puzzle that need to fit together," Aisha said. "We'll think about it later. Right now we need dinner and some rest."

"I'll prepare something special," Christy promised. "After all, we deserve a treat!"

Christy cooked a delicious meal. Everyone tried guessing the ingredients, but Christy kept shaking her head. They were all wrong. The only one thinking about something else was Aisha. The riddle was a difficult one.

Who knew what tomorrow would bring? After crossing the bridge she felt ready for almost anything and she was happy that all her friends were with her.

Day Three

After breakfast the next day, they headed for Grizzly Mountain. The road was more difficult than the previous day: sloping and falling, strewn with rocks and boulders. Since Sprint could not run as fast on that kind of land, Aisha asked Choo-Choo to check on the other groups.

In the meanwhile, Mabel decided to work on her band. Roy would be the trombone, Steven would play the bamboo flute, James would tap his feet to the beat and Yago would use his tail as a drum, since it was obvious he had a terrible voice. They were beginning to sound like a real rock group and Mabel was pleased.

A few hours passed and there was no sign of Choo-Choo. They finally found her still on the ground. Christy crawled rapidly towards her and realized that she wasn't hurt, except for her left wing. So while Christy prepared a healing brew for Choo-Choo's wing, she told her story.

"I was on my way back to you, when someone threw a stone at me. I think it was the cold-blooded group because the stone came right from where they were, but I can't be sure. And now, I can hardly fly," Choo-Choo added sadly.

"Not for some time," Christy said, "but you'll be fine if you put this on your wing and you don't move it for five days."

"Five days!" Choo-Choo shrieked. "But the competition will be over by then. What's the point in me going on with you? I might as well stay here or go back to school."

"No, Choo-Choo," Aisha said, "you've been a great help so far and we're all together in this. Nobody, and I repeat this, nobody will be left behind. All for one and one for all."

"Yes, Choo-Choo," Larry piped up, "you were great back on that bridge. I'd never have got across, if it wasn't for you. Hey! I can take you on my back."

"Thank you Larry," Choo-Choo said, "that's really nice of you!"

"So," Jumpy James asked, "now that you feel better, tell us how the other teams are doing."

"Well, the elephants finally decided to quit. They couldn't find a shallow part to cross the river. Besides, they'd take ages. The flying team already got to the Golden Tree and collected their stones, the felines are almost done collecting theirs, although it seems like they're always fighting, and the cold-blooded animals have one stone so far. The small animals group is behind the others and they're still trying to figure out how they'll climb the tree. It's far too tall and broad."

"Well," Aisha said, "let's go. We'll develop a strategy once we're there, just like we did at the bridge."

When they finally got to the Golden Tree, they saw the group of small animals returning. The team leader told Aisha that they had had a huge fight over how to get the stones, and eventually decided to go back. Aisha hoped her team would never fight like that. It was a competition among four teams now, since two had decided to quit. When they got to the Golden Tree, everyone realized why the small animals had fought so much.

The tree was really tall and wide and the branches were high. The small animals would've found it difficult to climb since there was nothing to hold on to. The stones were hanging like fruit, but they were so far up, that they would probably break if they were pulled down.

It was clear there was only one member in the group who could get the stones: Fani. One by one everybody turned to look at her.

It was so natural for her to be among the branches of a tree that for a moment, Fani forgot that it could have been a problem for somebody else. When Aisha asked her whether she could get the stones, she suddenly realized she could help and was thrilled.

"Of course I can," she said. "Easy does it."

Fani reached for the three beautiful stones and plucked them with ease. The yellow one had the shape of a heart, the green one was shaped like an olive leaf

and the purple one was a circle. They shone brightly. Aisha asked Steven to take care of the stones, since he was the most attentive in the group. Once he held them together in his hands, they heard a tiny beep from a pile of rocks nearby. On looking closely they noticed a small opening. Aisha was small enough to go in.

It was very dark inside but Aisha could see because she was glowing. She spied their envelope in a corner. Taking it, she went out again. Then she opened it among her friends and read:

"Head for the Magic Valley,
Singing a song as you rally."

"Where is the Magic Valley?" Croquie asked.

"Not far from here," Sprint said. "I've been there before. The road's easy and we can get there in two hours."

"Mabel will sing, obviously. Think of a good song, Mabel," Aisha said.

Sprint began to feel restless again on the way to the Valley. Christy, who was sprawled on his back then, noticed that something was wrong.

"Aisha, Sprint and I are going ahead to see if there are any obstacles. We'll be right back," she told Aisha. Then turning to Sprint she said, "Come on my friend, we're going for a ride."

Once they were well away from the rest of the group, Christy whispered, "Is something wrong, Sprint? You don't quite seem alright."

"I'm fine Christy. Why do you ask?" Sprint asked, touched at Christy's concern.

"I thought you looked a little blue, that's all. It used to happen to me often, so I notice when my friends have that feeling."

"Used to? Do you mean you don't feel blue anymore?" Sprint asked, interested.

"I'm diabetic as you know," Christy said. "It isn't as scary as it seems and I've learned a lot about nutrition and medicinal herbs, but back in Kindergarten my classmates wouldn't play with me because they thought it was contagious. I was miserable. But now, I realize that once I explain the disease, everybody understands. I can even cook healthy meals for everyone!"

"Wow," Sprint said, impressed. "Christy, you've been really helpful during this whole trip, making delicious, healthy meals for everyone and securing the

bridge at the fall, but I feel I've been completely useless. I didn't even help anybody across that bridge."

"So that's it," Christy said. "Don't worry Sprint, the competition isn't over yet and you're our best athlete. I'm sure your turn will come. Cheer up! Come on, run your best till the Magic Valley and we'll get back and report to the others."

They sped away. Sprint raced ahead smiling. He was beginning to feel good and he was grateful to Christy for cheering him up.

In the meantime, Mabel had composed a song. It was a cheery tune and the chorus went like this:

Yip yippy yimminny yay,
What a bright and sunny day,
Let's grab our coats and fly away,
And let's party all the way.

They had almost learned it by heart when Sprint and Christy got back and told everyone what they had seen. "The Magic Valley isn't too far away, but we'll have to cross a river to get to it."

They began to sing again as they marched. Christy winked at Sprint and he grinned. He decided to just relax and enjoy the walk.

When they got to the west side of Magic Valley, they saw the river they had to cross to get to the other side. It didn't look like a difficult river and they felt confident. Mabel however was not convinced. She looked anxiously into the depths of river and found, to her dismay, that she could not see the riverbed. Yago noticed immediately that Mabel was upset.

"What's the matter, Mabel?" he asked gently. "Are you worried about crossing the river?"

"Yes Yago, I can't help it," she said. "I've always been afraid of heights and rivers where I can't see the bed. I know I need to cross and I'm sure you'll all help me again, but it makes me so nervous I almost want to cry."

"Don't worry, Mabel dear," Yago said reassuringly. "We'll think of something. Why don't you get some rest now? You must be tired."

Mabel smiled, returned to the group and got ready to sleep. Everybody else had turned in by then. Croquie however, realized that Yago was missing. She went down to the shore to see if she could find him. Yago was still there, all by himself.

"What's the matter, Yago?" she asked.

"Oh Croquie," he said. "It's poor Mabel. She's afraid to cross the river and there must be something we can do about it."

"Do you have a plan?" Croquie asked.

"I'm going to build a dam," he replied. "It's what I do best. If I built a shallow, flat dam… then Mabel could wade through it. She'd be walking on something solid. That should comfort her."

33

"That's a great idea, Yago!" Croquie cried, clapping him on the back. "Can I help you?"

"Sure thing. Help me with some of those heavy logs floating in the river. I could use them to secure the dam."

"Alright! Let's get moving!" Croquie said as she jumped into the water. She felt happy inside the river, so light and full of energy. Together, they laid the logs end to end across the river and Yago built his dam on it. They went to sleep exhausted but very proud of what they had achieved that night.

Day Four

The first thing they saw when they woke the next morning was the dam.

"Hey!" James cried. "That wasn't there last night!"

When they found out that it was Yago and Croquie who built the dam, they cheered them. Mabel especially was really moved. She kissed Yago affectionately, her large brown eyes filing with tears of gratitude.

Sprint too was greatly relieved. He had an aversion to water and was impressed with how quickly Yago and Croquie had built the dam. "Good job, Croquie," he said warmly, as he passed her.

Croquie could barely believe it. Sprint, the best athlete in school! The same Sprint who'd always been so impatient with her, had actually congratulated her! Croquie's spirits soared.

They were all so happy, they started to cross the bridge singing the song Mabel had taught them. However when they were halfway across the bridge, a hawk suddenly appeared above them and dropped an envelope.

Aisha opened it and read it out aloud:

"Go to the Flat Wall
Don't pause or call
Just open the doors
For better or worse."

"Where on earth is the Flat Wall?" Fani asked.

"Can't say," said Aisha, "but I think it's somewhere close by. Let's just keep going."

On the way to Flat Wall, they saw the reptile group returning. They looked disappointed. Their leader said that the key to the test had apparently been strength and precision; they lacked the strength. It had been impossible for them

to open the doors, so they had decided to quit. He wished them good luck and told them the Flat Wall was just a few hundred meters ahead.

Once they got there, they understood its name. It was indeed a flat stone wall. It had three rounded holes, five feet apart from each other. Above the holes they could read the instruction, *"Push hard and strong on all the holes."*

"Hah!" that seems easy enough," James cried, pushing against the hole with all his might.

It remained firm.

"H'mm. That's strange. There's something funny about these hollows. Check it out, guys. Hey wait! Christy can check. She can slide easily into the hole," he said.

Christy came forward and slithered into the hole. Suddenly she stopped short.

She emerged a moment later looking slightly squashed.

"The holes curve upwards. They aren't straight. They're funny... like... like a rhino's horn!" she finished.

It was true. The hole was the perfect mould of a rhinoceros' horn. Everybody was fascinated.

Larry could do it! He could take a running leap and ram right into the holes. The doors would surely open then!

"Go on, Larry..." Aisha urged. "You're our only hope now."

Everybody moved aside to make way for Larry, who looked uneasy. He was rather fond of his horn and wasn't too pleased with the idea of risking it by thrusting it into a hole. It could get damaged. He did want to help out, but he was a little hesitant. After all, it was his crowning glory!

"I'd love to help," Larry said, "but I can't see very well and I'll have to run into the holes... right? What if my horn gets damaged?"

"Hey, don't worry," Choo-Choo said. "Remember what a great team we made, over at the bridge by the fall? Well, we can do that again. I'll be your eyes. C'mon on Larry! We can do this!"

"Alright, Choo," Larry said sounding reassured. "I'm still a little scared... but let's go."

Choo-Choo climbed on Larry's back and began to shout directions about the distance and the position, "ten feet, six feet, lower your head three inches, four feet, three feet, one more inch down, two feet, prepare your horn. Now!"

Larry lowered his head as he was told and charged straight at the hole. A loud noise was heard and a door appeared on the rock. The door was closed and there was no sign of a knob with which to open it.

"There's the first!" everyone cheered. "Yo, ho Larry, go Larry... c'mon on and show us Larry!

Then they went to the second line and Aisha gave them the signal to begin. A loud noise was heard again, and the second door appeared. But like the other one, it was shut.

Finally, they went to the third line. By now, Larry was rather enjoying himself. Besides, he could feel the power in his horn and knew it was strong. He almost laughed at himself for being so nervous.

They charged again. The third and final door appeared. And almost simultaneously, all three doors opened, as if by magic.

A turtle emerged out of each door, shell down.

Steven saw the envelope this time and handed it over to Aisha who read:

"The first is for wisdom,
The second for health.
The third is for love – untold wealth.
Use the stones – one in each,
Maybe then, you'll be well within reach."

"Alright, everybody put your thinking caps on. Any ideas?"

"Love is yellow," Croquie said. "Yellow's the color of the sun, and the sun warms us just like love warms our hearts. Besides, the wings of the yellow stone are shaped like a heart."

"Health is green," Christy said. "When trees are healthy, they put out green leaves and the green stone has the shape of a leaf."

"And Wisdom has to be the purple stone," Larry said. "It has the shape of a circle, with no beginning and no end. It's everlasting. Just like wisdom."

"Sounds good to me," Aisha said. "Anyone disagree?"

Nobody did. So Aisha asked Steven to place each stone on its respective turtle. Once the stones were arranged, the turtles disappeared; the doors shut by themselves and disappeared. For a while there was silence.

Eventually, a hyena came dashing towards them. He held an envelope gripped in his mouth. So they had been right after all!

The envelope simply read:

"Pay a visit...
Easy does it.
Have you the answer
For the Grandmaster?
Third key:
From the beginning, there is an end –
The purpose for which, one is really sent."

Day Five

Aisha was the first one up. She was always the first to wake. She had pondered endlessly about the three riddles. *You are beautiful the way you are.* They seemed so disconnected from each other. Yet, she was sure they were all linked. Some people were beautiful and others were really important. But what about the second clue? *Where you are... is where you should be.* And where would that be?

Almost instinctively, she thought: *here.*

But it couldn't be that simple. And if this really was a puzzle, the pieces simply did not seem to fit in together! Maybe she'd have to cut them to make them fit.

"O Wise Shaman," she thought aloud, "I wish you were here to help me."

She decided to wake the others up. If they were to call on the Grand Master, it would be wise to get there early. Besides, she knew that this would probably be the most difficult test so far.

They had a quick breakfast and set off immediately. They saw the flying team returning dejectedly.

Oh no! Aisha thought. Not another team eliminated. That meant it would be that much tougher for them.

"Hey Sprint," she called, "see if you can flag down their leader and ask them what happened."

Sprint darted off after them. Catching up with the birds, he yelled to them, hoping they'd hear him.

"Hey," he roared, "How come you guys are turning around?"

"Oh... it's a sad story," the Chief Bird said, halting in mid-air. "We got there before the felines. We were the first group and we thought were winning. However, when the Grandmaster received us in his cottage, he opened a huge book and asked us who had been the three most famous discoverers in Africa. We had no idea. We know everything about flying and pilots, but discoverers are land-birds," he said sadly. "We did try the Wright Brothers, though," he added. "We're in third place now. That means the bronze medal. Ah well. Anyway... good luck to you guys."

Sprint thanked them and bade them farewell. He was shocked. He had no idea about the discoverers; he only knew about sports and athletes. But discoverers and discoveries? This was going to be an extremely difficult test, and he hoped someone in the group would know the answers.

He dashed back to join the group. They were laughing and having a whale of a time. It had to be another of Fani's funny stories, he thought. He decided not to join them immediately since he didn't want to ruin their fun.

So he waited till Fani was done telling her story and then burst in, pretending to be breathless.

He quickly told them what the flying team had said.

"Livingstone had to be one of them," Steven shouted instantly. "I'm sure."

"But I'm sure the Grandmaster won't ask the same question to two different teams," Aisha said.

When they arrived at the Grandmaster's cottage they saw no sign of the felines. That meant they had passed the test and had already gone ahead of them.

Aisha knocked softly and a deep voice told her to enter. The entire team trooped in. It was a pleasant little cottage, with bright flowers in colored glasses on the little ledges everywhere. There were thick heavy books crammed into the shelves. The Grandmaster, a monstrous looking toad, told them they had arrived

just in time. He had choir practice with the other frogs in Webber's Pond, in an hour's time.

"So," the Grandmaster began, "you are here to answer some questions. These questions are based on general knowledge. So I hope you've all been paying attention in class. Shall we begin then?"

The Grandmaster was an enormous toad with plenty of warts. He had a magnificent bubble at his throat that seemed to swell as he puffed out his words. But he seemed a jovial sort and they were not too intimidated.

"Yes, sir," Aisha said. "But we'd really appreciate it if you allowed us to discuss our answers before we gave them to you. That's always been our way of working."

"That's good," the Grandmaster said with a smile, "come outside. I like your name, Aisha," he said suddenly. "Do you know what it means?"

Aisha was surprised. "But how..." she began. "No... I don't. Please tell me."

"Oh, I know all of you," the Grandmaster said. "I've been around for a long time. Your name means 'life'. Either you can discuss the question before answering or appoint someone to answer. But only one person must answer, not three at a time as in the previous group. Well," he said after a brief pause, "here's my first question: Which is the longest river in the world, and the longest in China?"

Aisha liked geography. She knew the longest river in the world was the Nile, but she didn't know about China. She turned to Steven. He was smiling.

"You answer Steve," she whispered. "The longest river in the world is the Nile."

Steven gave the answers promptly. "The Nile and the Yangtze," he said.

"That's right," the Grandmaster said. "It's a good thing you picked a representative, Aisha," he said. "I approve. The previous group picked a quarrel because too many of them wanted to answer at the same time."

"Now for the other question: Name the deepest lake and the highest peak in the world."

Aisha knew Mt. Everest in Asia was the highest peak and she knew that in Africa, Lake Tanganyika, about 1435 meters deep, was the deepest. But was it the deepest in the world? Steven said it was Lake Baikal in Asia. It had to be. It was over 1600 meters deep.

So Steven gave the answers again. And he was right.

"Perfect!" said the Grandmaster with a big smile. "Congratulations. Here is your envelope. Good luck. Now if you'll all excuse me, I have a choir session to attend."

Aisha read out the note in the envelope as they all filed out of the Grandmaster's cozy little cottage. The message read:

"On to Shanty Island to find the gem,
The Keepers of the Stone guard its helm,
Once you have it, a minute you'll get –
Hand it over, in the Valley of the Bed."

"Where's Shanty Island?" Sprint asked.

"It is in the middle of the Rippling River," Croquie said. "I know the way... it's up north."

It was already dusk by the time they arrived.

The river was unusually wide, and right in the middle of it was a small island. Ranged round the shore was a band of fierce looking vultures and wolves – the Guardians of the Stone. There appeared to be a party of some sort on; much merry-making and rollicking; nobody seemed to be really paying attention to the jewel, which was in a shining box in the middle.

Somebody suddenly spotted the feline group slinking away. They seemed to have given up. Aisha hailed their leader, who told her that after much infighting they had decided it was impossible for them to cross such a wide river, and had indeed given up.

Aisha returned to her group. "It's just us now, folks. All the other teams have dropped out. So if we don't make it past this, it'll be a repeat of last year: A no-result outcome. We can't let that happen!"

"Let me go Aisha," Croquie piped up. "I'm the only one who can get there, since Choo-Choo can't fly yet."

"That's true, but it's too dangerous for you to go alone." Aisha said.

"There's no other way. I'm fine as long I'm in the water," said Croquie. "The trouble is, the box is right in the midst of them. And I'll have to crawl ashore to get it. I'm afraid I'll mess up once I'm out of the water."

"We'll have to distract them, then," said James, "while Croquie gets the jewel."

"I know!" Mabel put in, "Let's sing a song to distract them. The whole band can join in."

"No. Let's insult them and yell at them to make them angry," said Yago.

"We'll do something. In the meantime, Sprint can lie in wait for Croquie to return with the jewel. Then he can sprint off as fast as he can to the Valley of the Bed."

"The Valley of the Bed? That's a strange name. Where is it?" Sprint asked.

"I know. I thought so too. If it's possible to get there in a minute, it should be close by. In fact, I have a sneaky suspicion that it's that Valley full of flowers over there." Aisha pointed to a valley behind her. "Bed of flowers! That has to be it!"

"JJ, I need you to go to that tree and cut some coconuts. If they attack us, Roy can help us throwing them with his trunk. To begin with, all of us will try to distract them in different ways," she continued.

Everybody agreed and took their places. Sprint and Croquie headed towards the island, after making sure the vultures and wolves were not looking. Croquie jumped into the water as soon as the group began to make noises to draw the attention of the guardians.

The vultures were laughing really hard because they could see what a weird group they were.

"What a pathetic group!" they said mocking them. "Why don't you just give up?"

In making fun of Aisha's group, the guardians had forgotten about the box in their midst. They had all ranged themselves along the shore to peer and jeer at Aisha's strange team.

Croquie crept out of the water, as quietly as she could and crawled towards the glittering box. Taking the box, she made her way back towards the shore of the island, inching along painfully. But she took so long getting back, that one of the vultures happened to spy her creeping away with the treasure.

He shouted for his mates to follow. "Hey," he hollered. "That crocodile's making off with the Jewel. Let's get her boys!"

But it was too late. Croquie was already in the water... and once in the water, she was off like a torpedo.

They began to fly after her. The wolves hopped on to a piece of driftwood, which they used as a raft to follow her.

Croquie immediately ducked and the vultures lost sight of her. In the meantime JJ and Yago began to pelt the approaching wolves with coconuts. Roy launched them into the air with his trunk... straight at the vultures.

The vultures were having a difficult time avoiding the coconuts, when suddenly Croquie resurfaced and lashed at the raft behind her, with her powerful tail. Sprint was surprised to see how well Croquie was doing. She had reached the shore in a matter of seconds and handed over the jewel to Sprint.

"Hurry up, Sprint!" she said. "We only have one minute and those evil guardians are right behind me."

"Just watch me, Croquie," Sprint said as he flew off.

Once the guardians saw that the jewel had been given to Sprint, who was off in a flash, they decided to give up the chase and return to their island.

The rest of the group walked towards the Valley of the Bed congratulating Croquie. However, they were all worried about Sprint. He was a great runner, but would he make it in time? Suddenly Choo-Choo began to shout, "He's coming! I see him! I see Sprint coming back! He made it!"

Sprint had indeed made it in record time and rejoined the group. He held an envelope in his mouth. Everybody cheered and shouted because that meant they had almost made it. There was just one test to go!

Sprint was congratulated all round but he said warmly, "We'd never have done it without Croquie's help; she is such a great swimmer!"

"Really Croquie," he told her later, "you made it look so easy, you're so graceful in the water. It almost seemed like you were sprinting. I'm sorry I've been mean. I just did not know what a great athlete you were."

Aisha was the happiest of them all, because finally all her friends were getting along perfectly.

"Attention everybody," she called, "We're almost there. The envelope says *'Go to the Palace of Wonders and give the answer to the keys'.* Remember, we haven't got too far with the keys yet. So we'll have to work on that."

Although they were worried about the Final Test the next day, they decided to enjoy their last dinner together, chuckling over their first impressions of each other. They did want to win but they were simply overjoyed at having got this far together. It was more than they had expected.

45

Sitting around a bonfire, singing picnic songs about the thousand legged worm, Aisha suddenly thought of the Wise Shaman and realized how wise he had been when he had told her to follow her heart. She was happy now, amongst all her friends, and well, they had done rather well, hadn't they?

Day Six

The little group set off early the next morning. They felt more relaxed now that they did not have to watch out for the other teams. However the three riddles still weighed heavily on Aisha's mind. She repeated them over and over again to herself, hoping to make some sense of it.

"You are beautiful the way you are.
Where you are... is where you should be.
From the beginning, there is an end –
The purpose for which, one is really sent."

When they arrived at the Palace of Wonders, all the other animals were waiting for them. They were applauding them for having triumphed over all the challenges thrown at them so far. But everybody knew that the competition was far from over. There was still one more test to go – the Final Test.

The main judges arrived eventually and seated themselves in the center of a magnificent podium, in the front yard of the Palace of Wonders.

Once the formalities had been dispensed with, the oldest judge addressed Aisha.

"Well Aisha," he said, "your group has almost made it. But to win, you must now answer the three riddles. I can give you just one clue: the answer to all of them is the same, and it is just one word."

Aisha was stunned. The answer to all those keys was just one word? That was crazy! Being group leader, it was her responsibility to be the spokesperson of her group. She knew they would support her, regardless of the answer, but she was nervous. She looked at the crowd and saw her mother, who placed her hand on her heart, as if to remind her of the Wise Shaman's words. That little gesture calmed Aisha down, and she tried to be really still to be able to hear her heart if it spoke to her.

She thought about the members of her group and the competition. Mabel was beautiful; but so was Fani when she was telling stories, Choo-Choo when she was flying, Croquie when she was swimming, or Sprint when he was running. She knew her own purpose so far had been to put the group together, but there had also been a purpose in Christy's illness and her special knowledge, and Larry's horn. Each one of them had saved the situation at some point during the competition, so if even one of them had not been there, they could never have made it. All of them had been needed. Each and...

Suddenly, Aisha saw the answer very clearly. It had been so obvious; she had almost missed it! With a big smile she turned to the judges. A sudden hush fell over the crowd.

"Everyone," she said.

Pin-drop silence as the crowd waited for the judges' response.

The oldest judge turned to look at her gravely... and then slowly, very slowly, as if to prolong the crowd's agony, he said, "The answer is... correct!"

A mighty whoop of victory went up from Aisha's team. There was hugging and crying and cheering all round. The crowd exploded. Confetti balls, little streamers and balloons were sent up into the air. The sky was aflame with the colors of celebrations.

The judges waited for silence to settle, before they began again.

"The main purpose of this competition has always been to identify future leaders. We do not need leaders who only want to destroy their enemies or use violence to achieve their ends. We need leaders who try to understand that every single one is important and make teamwork possible. The odds were in favor of Aisha's group right from the beginning because she included those with different

abilities. She did not go only for the strongest, fastest or the most intelligent. However, the other groups had their chances too. The problem was that they decided to fight rather than to cooperate."

"So, young leaders," he continued as he stepped down and put a crown of leaves on Aisha's head, "your group has taught us a great lesson. Let's not forget we are all brothers and sisters and that Africa is our home. There is uniformity even in our diversity."

Once he had placed an olive crown on every member of the group he added, "The Palace of Wonders will be opened for Aisha and her group so they can receive special training required to become the leaders of tomorrow and now..." he added quite unexpectedly, with a wink that only a few could see distinctly, "now, let's party."

"But what about the prize?" asked Choo-Choo, a little troubled. "We already have it," replied Aisha. "We found friendship and discovered ourselves. What's more, we're going to be the leaders of tomorrow."

And so the party began. Each of the team members celebrated in their own way: Mabel sang while Yago drummed (with his tail) though he sorely lacked a

sense of rhythm. Roy danced, taking care not to step on anybody's toes. Sprint and Croquie organized a new kind of land-and-water competition. Choo-Choo and Larry made arrangements to study and play together, just like JJ and Steven had done. Fani was in the center of a spellbound group, narrating the whole adventure. Christy was surrounded by those who loved the delicious food she dished out.

And as for Aisha, she went to pay the Wise Shaman a visit, to thank him and tell him what he already knew. That he had been right all along.

CHILDREN'S BOOKS FROM UNISUN

Little Santa

An adventure for the young and old,
A Christmas story - brave and bold,
Of a child whose concern and care,
Saved the world from black despair.
Celebrating for all the right reasons,
This the most marvellous of seasons.

ISBN 81-88234-06-0 - Sp. Indian price: Rs. 99/-

Noah the Friendly Computer Virus
A modern-day fantasy that will warm your heart. Noah a computer virus, hates his job. He yearns for the simple pleasures of life we take for granted - family, friends and a life you can call your own. Robin a ten-year-old tries to rescue Noah and give him a chance.... An exciting adventure told with verve and vigour... combining the latest technology with the most timeless of human values. A story for every parent and every child... for the computer geek and the incurable romantic
"(The author) has her fingers well placed on the pulse of the changing times."-The New Indian Express
"A swift paced story of courage and comradeship, laced with wholesome humor. Noah will certainly worm his way into your affections." - *Deccan Herald*

ISBN 81-88234-13-3 - Sp. Indian price: Rs. 99/-

Noah to the Rescue
Noah the friendly computer virus has long escaped the claustrophobic confines of the computer and found the partner of his dreams. But their idyllic happiness is threatened by an outbreak of avian flu in faraway Thailand.
A heartwarming book, about the enduring values of friendship and sacrifice.
A book that seamlessly weaves together, the intricacies of science and the complexities of the human heart.
"Noah to the Rescue mixes science, reality and fantasy to make an exciting concoction." - *Deccan Herald*

ISBN 81-88234-08-7 - Sp. Indian price: Rs. 99/-

Spinning Sunshine
A little boy who is so attached to his computer that he begins to turn into one, a farmer who faces the warth ot the sun god when he nearly sets his field on fire, the spider Anansi who is chased into the shadows, the little old lady who sneezed her teeth across the country's border...

These are stories from across the world. They include folk-tales from Africa and the Navajos of America, as well as fiction from Never-never land. These are stories that spread the spirit of the sun - energy, warmth, the life giving force - around which our earth revolves.
Tales to warm the cockles of your heart.

ISBN 81-88234-01-X - Sp. Indian price: Rs. 60/-

Ganesha - ancient stories for modern times

- a serpentine foe is taught a timely lesson...
- a succulent mango produces inspired thinking...
- a brother's romance requires a helping hand...
- a stringent diet produces dramatic results...
- a passing whim invites a father's wrath...

When Ganesha, the Remover of Obstacles, is around, there is no dearth of fun or excitement.

Recounted by an all-too-earthly scribe, this heavenly collection of stories about the loveable elephant-headed god is irresistible.

By turns reverent and irreverent, traditional and contemporary, the author ensures that these ageless stories remain relevant to our times.

ISBN 81-88234-15-X - Sp. Indian price: Rs. 125/-

The Lion who wanted to sing and other stories

Walk into a forest where the animals are all too human.
Leo, the lion king who becomes vegetarian for a purpose.
Waggle, the worm who keeps his word.
Kiara, the elephant who cannot bear to look into the mirror.

Lively stories you cannot resist.
A book that advocates determination, perseverance, integrity, friendship, kindness, sacrifice…
And teaches you to be yourself.
A read-aloud book for parents and their tiny tots.

ISBN 81-88234-14-1 - Sp. Indian price: Rs. 125/-

Bunny in search of a name and other stories

Meet
Bunny, the baby rabbit who hates his own name.
Paru, the parrot who pays for her pride.
Casca, the crow who pretends to be what he is not.
And the chaos that results when the Wishing Fairy grants every animal his wish!

Imaginative stories that entertain and teach.
A book that teaches you to be yourself, to value friendship and honesty.
A read-aloud book for parents and their tiny tots.

ISBN 81-88234-18-4 - Sp. Indian price: Rs. 125/-

Doogoo the noisy elephant and other stories

Doogoo the baby elephant travels from Heggada Devana Kote to the USA.
Hooter the owl protects his little friends in the apartment block.
Manju the masterful monkey makes his master a prince.

Malavika Kapur, psychologist and environmentalist, teaches us the importance of co-existence... in the jungles and cities.

ISBN 81-88234-16-8 - Sp. Indian price: Rs. 125/-